We Obedient Children

———

We Obedient Children

Karris Rae

Etchings Press
University of Indianapolis
Indianapolis, Indiana

This publication is made possible by funding provided by the Shaheen College of Arts and Sciences and the Department of English at the University of Indianapolis. Special thanks to the students who judged, edited, designed, and published this chapbook: Abby Bailey, Liza Harris, and Amber Phillips.

UNIVERSITY *of*
INDIANAPOLIS.

Published by Etchings Press
1400 E. Hanna Ave.
Indianapolis, Indiana 46227
All rights reserved

etchings.uindy.edu
www.uindy.edu/cas/english

Printed by IngramSpark

Published in the United States of America

ISBN 978-1-955521-35-2
28 27 26 25 24   1 2 3 4 5

Cover art by Alloria Watson

Table of Contents

For Mama and Grandma Luc,
whose roots are interwoven with mine.
May our roses prosper together.

Μέδουσα

[The Guardian]

Poseidon conquered the priestess of the virgin goddess as the watching roses closed their many eyes. Then he left the temple quickly, not for fear of consequence, but to escape the cloying smell of the night-wary flowers. The cobbled streets were quiet. The mortals slept in cramped houses under red-tiled roofs. Poseidon wondered how many of the dreaming women were as beautiful as the priestess, whose name he did not know.

(Medusa lay curled on the stone floor. The cool tiles mercifully numbed her skin as if drawing out a fever.)

Poseidon followed the road as it wound down the steep hillside, down to the sea where his kingdom waited for its master. When he reached the water he let the ocean kiss his toes. Gentle, glassy waves rolled and broke before him as if afraid to be seen. He was pleased.

(She lay still as death until a battle-hardened hand lit upon her naked shoulder. "This will never happen again," her patron whispered. "I promise.")

As he waded into the surf, he saw something in the water. An afterimage, an echo, a memory of a lovely face before the bruising and bitten lips. The wave collapsed before he could study it.

(The scent of roses clung to her unclothed body. Medusa, who had nothing more to fear, saw him silhouetted by moonlight and smiled.)

The wave rose again and there was her reflection, closer now, the woman without a name. As perfect as when he first touched her, unbroken again. Poseidon turned to face the priestess on the beach. He saw then what she'd become. As he was seized by horror, his godly reflexes took hold—he assumed the form of a giant crab with a protective shell as hard as stone.

(She saw the fear in his eyes before he turned into marble, gray-blue like the ocean before the rain.)

Poseidon's shell crackled as it calcified. The affliction crept joint by joint, the juices within turning cold and still. Before the liquid in his eyes turned to sightless, milky quartz, Poseidon saw pity in the monster's cursed gaze.

(Medusa did pity him—but not enough.)

The monster left. The waves broke defiantly over Poseidon's eight pointed toes. He didn't see the sun break, but he did feel the first rays.

Suddenly, a touch—so light that Poseidon almost confused it for sunlight. A clawed finger traced the lines in his carapace. Its caress shivered with a hiss, a hush. *Don't touch me*, Poseidon thought. But he could not articulate the plea.

(Medusa had begged, too.)

The monster shoved something hard and blunt between the plates of Poseidon's marbled shell. He did not see the hammer poised to strike, but he felt the bite of the chisel. Gods do not often suffer pain. They feel it the way an infant does—unable to imagine it ever ending, to remember a past before it began.

The first piece broke from his body and fell to the

sand. Then another, sounding like fat raindrops. Bit by bit, his blocky carapace became a spindly waist and a ripely rounded abdomen. All his divine might of will, and Poseidon couldn't even curl up to protect his weakest parts. The monster started on his face next, digging out his eye stalks, his mouth pieces.

(Medusa saw the eight eyes and the pedipalps hiding in his face and carved out everything else. Shards of the king's face littered his beach, the threshold of his domain. She examined her work, crab to spider, angles to curves, Ares to Aphrodite. When she spoke, she pressed her lips against Poseidon's skin. Her breath fogged the cool marble.)

"Now, you are one of us. A victim. A monster. But this is not the end. Please, take this chance to transform into something better." With inhuman strength and human grace, Medusa lifted the marble spider statue and carried it to the temple of her rebirth. There, she placed it in a dark corner, praying to Athena that the statue's many eyes would scare ill-meaning men away.

(The blind god inside was not blessed with a last glimpse of his ocean.)

And in his absence, the moon, gentle Selene, would reclaim her jewel-bright seas and never let them go.

貞子

[The Chaste Child]

When Tahira first recommends that you watch the Japanese original of *The Ring*, you say she's crazy for liking that freaky stuff. You've never understood the appeal of surrendering to fear for fun. Fear is scary. You prefer fast-paced movies about muscled heroes doing what they want and always, *always* winning in the end.

But then came that rumsick night, and the miscommunication, and now you guys don't talk much anymore. You're not sure how things went wrong, or how it's your fault when she's the one who changed her mind. Sometimes you want to ask others in the crew what they think, but you always stop before you get to the heart of the question. Everyone knows that alcohol fuels fires, yet somehow, everyone's always surprised when things ignite.

So tonight you're bored, stoned, and alone (with increasing frequency, these days). You're in the rare mood to watch one of the movies you promised to see years ago, and look at that—you can stream *Ringu* for free. So you do.

And what a movie, fuck.

What is *up* with that doctor? The guy rapes the ghost girl (Sadako—before she's a ghost, obviously), then finds out afterward that she's hermaphroditic and kills her for it. But like, if he's worried sleeping with a pretty ladyboy makes him gay, it's kinda too late. That's not in the American version, and you're worried for any country where this is mainstream entertainment.

The credits roll and you have so many things to say. You're formulating the witty, bullet-pointed text you're going to send Ben when your back pocket vibrates. Unlisted number on your smartphone screen, probably a scammer. But you're waiting to hear back from the clinic and don't know their number, so you answer.

"You will die in seven days."

You nearly drop the phone, heart pounding. Then you manage a word: "Tahira?"

The young woman on the other end giggles. "NoOo, I'm SadakOoO." You can imagine her wiggling her fingers theatrically, wherever she is.

"Hey," you say. "How'd you know I was watching it?"

"Ben said so."

"Dammit. Guy never keeps his mouth shut, does he?"

"Not for his life."

You force a laugh, hoping she'll keep speaking. Maybe if she keeps talking like normal, you can keep being friends like normal. But she waits for you.

"So what's up?" you ask. "It's been a while since we last—"

"Shit, I gotta go. Talk to you later. And don't forget! *You will die in seven days.*" She hangs up.

You usually have nightmares after watching horror movies, but this one gets you bad. It's not awful in the daytime, but you realize on day three that you've been leaving the hall light on overnight. You avoid walking past the living room to pee. You don't like the way the TV screen blurs out your reflection beyond recognition, like police cam footage scrambled to protect suspects' identities. Sometimes Netflix asks if you're still watching, and when you press "yes," there's a half-frame of black that you come to fear.

In that half-second, it's not Sadako you see, but Tahira.

You're extra edgy on the seventh day, but you're in luck—it's a Saturday. So instead of hanging around your apartment waiting for Sadako to crawl through the TV and stuff you in a closet, you meet Ben at the bar. You drink too many whiskey sours and tongue a chubby blonde in the corner near the emergency exit. There aren't even any Asian chicks there.

You survive.

The blonde calls you back the next day. At first you think it's the weird unlisted number Tahira called from, but it's one digit off. You realize you're disappointed. You ignore it.

The day after, Ben cancels the weekly movie night. He says he feels "crappy," and you tell him to keep his crap to himself. You regret polishing off his old-fashioned when he wasn't looking—then again, alcohol kills germs. You offer to host movie night instead, but no one in the group chat responds. Though you're hypervigilant of cold and flu symptoms, you don't get sick.

The next week, Ben and Caitlin are busy studying for an exam. The week after that, no one mentions the movie night at all. Gradually, the group chat slows and then stops, until one day there's a notification: "Tahira has left the chat."

Your phone buzzes and shows a familiar number. Your heart pounds, expecting Tahira's voice, but it's just the blonde again. You guys meet at your place and smoke and fuck. She asks you to choke her and you do, pushing her into the bed as if holding her head underwater. Even when her resistance turns to desperate clawing, you don't stop until you finish. She does not speak to you as she collects her clothes and leaves. Why? Wasn't that what she wanted?

Days pass, Ben calls. He is plastered out of his skull, voice husky and raucous.

"Tahira's dead, man."

No preamble. You hear soft voices in the background, though Ben must be yelling into the phone. "What?"

"Yup, killed herself this morning. Left a note. No fucking way I'm reading it, but Caitlin won't shut up about it." He laughs erratically. Ben would never think to be this cruel if it weren't true—if grief weren't forcing his mind into strange shapes. "She basically saved me the trouble. You know what she's telling people?"

"What?" you say, licking your lips.

"She's saying you *raped* Tahira. I knew something fucky happened between you guys, but rape, dude? What the hell."

You find an excuse to hang up on Ben. As soon as you do, you wish he was still there, talking over your thoughts. So they think you're a rapist. Like that guy in the movie—that doctor. But you'd never do something like that. Caitlin should know better.

Tahira's Facebook page corroborates her death. Post after post, happy pictures with friends, her mom, her niece and nephew. One of the pictures was taken the night you last saw her, before the crew took off and left you two alone. Her hair smelled like shampoo that night. Something floral—a flower you can't place.

Your mind bends into strange shapes now, too. You can't sleep. You get out of bed and turn on the hall light.

Back in bed, the mattress is soft under you and you're sinking, unable to breathe. The sheets smell like flowers, and the next day you buy new laundry detergent. When you brush your teeth there are spiders in the sink and you wash them down the drain. When you rifle through your notepad, the words all blur except your name.

Days pass. You're so tired, so tired, so tired, so tired. Shadows creep at the edges of your vision. You dust the corners and spiders scramble out of the way, into deeper crevices in your home. You're afraid to put your shoes on or reach into dark drawers. You know the spiders are waiting for you there. They're watching you.

Sometimes, when you pass your bedroom, you think there's dark hair splashed out on your pillow. It always disappears when you look right at it, but the rosy scent left on your pillows perfumes your half-dreams. You keep the door closed. This is worse, because it means the hair never goes away.

Seven days after Tahira's suicide, you drag yourself to bed, though you know it won't help. The hair drapes over your cream pillows and sheets, and tonight, it doesn't vanish when you fix your gaze. You reach toward it, too tired to tremble, and hook your finger around the black curls. Tahira is staring at you, unblinking, livid. You try to turn, to leave, to undo, but her hand shoots out from under the blanket and seizes your wrist. Icy legs and arms wrap around you. Didn't you want this? She ties you into a knot around herself, one shattered bone at a time. When she's done, your combined eight limbs hang over the edges of the bed, and all the little spiders find refuge under the blankets with you.

Cailín

[The Girl]

The girl had always wanted a rose like her mother's. Her mother's rosebush had grown from a small cutting of her mother's, whose roses grew from her grandmother's, and so on, all the way back to England. Or so it was said. The blossoms were round and full like heads of cabbage, so heavy that the fragile stems bowed. Blush pink skin closed over dewy, ruby insides.

No one grows these anymore, her mother once said. *Just us.*

And for good reason—the roses had always been sickly. From the cradle, the girl helped her mother mash the spiders that plagued the rosebush and fed on the gentle bugs that lived between the petals. But they always came back.

The only time the flowers ever thrived was around their owners' deaths. The family learned not to attempt cuttings outside these times. And so, without realizing it, the girl was waiting for her mother to die.

Right before her eighteenth birthday, the girl got her cutting. After her mother's funeral, she dug a hole in the field behind the house and planted her stem over her mother's grave, barely more than a stick with a single flower. She listed every rule her mother had taught her about the care of roses. She pinned it to the wall above her vanity mirror so she'd never forget. Every morning she woke up with the sun to weed and hunt down spiders while the dew still gilded their webs. *Every other bush may have sickened*, she thought. *But not mine.*

Still, the vibrant stem turned yellow and mushy. The rotten outer layers of the blossom peeled away, exposing sick flesh within. The gentle bugs took refuge inside the rose's deepest layers and refused to come out where the spiders waited.

The girl told herself that it could not be helped, after all. If her love for her mother wasn't enough to nourish the flowers, then nothing could. But still, as she knelt before her mother's grave, beneath her withering rose, she could not quell the feeling that she had failed the woman buried there.

The girl redoubled her efforts, crushing horrid spiders until the sun bore down. Until a spider, who could not bear to see any more of her sisters murdered, bit. The girl had barely registered the pain when she collapsed in the dirt.

She woke up in agony with venom corroding her veins. When she spoke, her father, sitting at her bedside, raised his head. His face was flushed and glistening with anxious sweat, but he smiled and wrapped her in his arms.

I thought I was going to lose you, too.

The girl buried her head in his shoulder. She was not yet certain that his fears had been proven wrong. She hurt down to the marrow in her bones; every muscle resisted her command.

But she did not die. Not yet. Almost every day, she suffered a little less. On clear days, she would have her father open the curtains looking out over the back field, and could see her single rose raising its magnificent head to the sky. At first she wondered if this meant that her recovery was illusory, that she would one day lapse into motionlessness when her father looked away. But still, she lived.

The first time she felt strong enough to leave the house, she, with her father's assistance, shuffled out to where her rose grew. She was not yet within ten feet of it before she could smell its perfume. Weeds and vines had wrapped around its feet, anchoring it firmly to the ground. Spiders had woven webs out of silver thread between the blossom and the yearning leaves. Without the girl's misguided care, the spiders had protected the rosebush from the beetles eating it from the inside, and the weeds had allowed the roots to take firm hold.

The girl knelt, wishing she knew how to apologize in the language of spiders. But as she watched them tirelessly spin their thread, she sensed that she was already forgiven.

Santa Rita

[The Pearl Saint]

"O Holy Patroness of the abused and afraid, Santa Rita, who for thy lavishness in granting favors hast been called the Advocate of the hopeless . . . By thy heroic sufferings during thy married life, by the sacrifice of thy children rather than see them grievously offend God, and by the severe penances and thrice daily scourgings . . . obtain for me my request."

I say this in Spanish, squinting to decipher my Tía's strange handwriting. I bow my head and pray silently in English: "Please, Saint Rita, protect me from Sofia."

I lift my eyes to meet Santa Rita's. Her face is carved into an expression of profound love. It bothers me to know it's the same look she'd give Sofia. At the Lady's stone feet I lay a rose, her flower, amongst dozens of others, and then I leave the shrine. My Tía would cluck her tongue at my timidity. That's why I asked that she stay home. I also didn't want to listen to her suck her teeth for the three-hour drive.

I cross the parking lot to my car, turn it on, and pull out of the lot. I should be nicer to Tía. She's all I have now, after I had the audacity to bring Sofia to Thanksgiving. Yeah yeah, God loves everyone—except the dykes. So then, when one dyke goes nuts on the other, there's not much a good Catholic can do but shrug. Tía at least gave me a prayer.

On the drive home, I stop at a gas station to buy a can of Red Bull. My breath solidifies in my throat when I see who's manning the front register. She has a spider's face. Tiny glittering eyes like a crown of black pearls. Hairy, powerful pedipalps flexing, fangs tucked underneath. The nametag pinned to her polo identifies her as "Betty." Somehow I know she's looking at me. I slowly back up and let the door automatically close between us. As soon as I'm out of sight, I'm running, wrenching my door open and throwing the shift into drive. I don't make any more stops.

Now at home, I make enchilada casserole with store-bought sauce (cluck cluck) and crawl into bed. My phone is in my hand and it's so tempting to look, though I know I won't like what I see. Yes, Sofia's there in the front door security camera. Against the amber, light-polluted sky, I see the pencil tucked behind her ear. She clutches a notepad to her chest.

Feeling brave, I down the water in the plastic cup on my bedside table and throw it. It clatters on the hardwood floor and Sofia's silhouette jerks. She removes the pencil and dutifully notes the disturbance. I wish she'd turn into a spider. Make her outsides match her insides.

For eight hours, I fail to sleep. I rouse myself for work, dragging myself into the shower, out, into the car, out, into the building. As I cross the lobby, I'm bowed over my phone screen, expecting the room to be deserted. The receptionist, Fiona, has been on unpaid leave the past week. Rumor is, she finally told the boss to keep his hands to himself.

"Hey, Margarita! Feels like I haven't seen you in forever." Fiona's voice startles me.

When I look up, surprise turns to horror. There's another spider in the receptionist's chair, mouth parts working to clean shiny black fangs as it reschedules a client.

"Have a good weekend?" it says, with Fiona's midwestern accent.

I dart back outside. Leaning against the brick exterior, I breathe so hard and fast my lungs ache. "Please, Santa Rita. Protect me from these monsters."

I return to my car, my face bloodless and numb. The reflection I see in the rearview mirror is unnerving, familiar shapes contorted into something I don't recognize. It's too easy to imagine extra eyes and fangs there. So easy that I wonder if the people passing by my car see them too, or if it's only visible to those who know to look.

A rap on the passenger window startles me. Adrenaline jolts down into my fingers. On the other side is another spider person, a man wearing grass-stained cargo shorts.

"You okay in there?" he asks.

I bury my face in my hands. There's nowhere else to go. "Please go away."

He steps back. "Okay, ma'am. I'm just doing some landscaping out here, so if you need anything, just let me know. My name's Frank."

He leaves without asking for my name. His footsteps retreat and give way to the sound of a weed whacker. I sit there for a half hour before something occurs to me—I slip my phone out and dial Tía's number. She answers on the second ring.

"Tía? It's Margarita."

"Ah! My baby Margarita," she says in Spanish. "You're safe, yes? No trouble?"

"No, it's not like that." We each wait for the other to speak. Tía is more patient than me. "I went to Santa Rita's shrine yesterday like you said."

"Good girl. Santa Rita has helped me with many troubles. I'm sure she will help you, too."

"Have you ever seen anything after asking her? Like . . . spidery things?"

Tía laughs. "I guess you did not ask to see spidery things?"

"Hell no, I didn't."

"Watch your mouth, Margarita." Tía's voice softens again. "I do not know, my girl. But whatever the reason, the Lady must know that's what you need."

There's another sharp knock on the driver's side window, and I wave it away irritably before I look up. It's not Frank, but Sofia, and she is still not a spider. Her teeth are set so fiercely that I'm surprised they haven't cracked.

"Tía. I'll call you back." How did Sofia get here?

Sofia is trembling. "Now you listen to me. I am suffering. But you know what's worse than living without you? Knowing that you're suffering even more, and not being able to help." She digs through her pockets, pulls out a wad of folded notes. She rifles through them until she finds the right one, then slaps it against my windshield. "I hear you pacing late at night, and it takes everything in me not to come in and hold you."

12:42—clattering from front bedroom. She's still not sleeping well.

"I love you, and I know you love me too." At her side is a wrench.

"Alright, Sofia." My mouth is dry. "Let's talk."

"Let me in the car."

"I can hear you just fine like this."

Sofia strikes the side of the car with the wrench. "You obviously fucking can't, since you just keep taking off as soon as things get hard, like you always do. I'm getting in the fucking car."

She is going to beat me to death in my own vehicle. The thought appears in plain black and white, like text on my eyelids.

"Everything good here?" I didn't hear the weed whacker or the footsteps stop but here is Frank, fangs poised. His many eyes see the dented metal and the web of cracks in the window.

Sofia nods cheerily. Whatever she thinks of his pedipalps, she does not say.

"Are you sure?" he asks. "It kind of looks to me like everything is not good. You should get on home, lady. This parking lot is for employees only."

Sofia, still breathing hard, looks at him, at me, at the car. At the wrench. "Guess you'll have to fix your own car," she finally chirps, her voice and face discordant. "See you later, baby." She stalks off around the side of the building.

"Wouldn't go into work today, if I were you," Frank says. "Bet anything she's hiding around the corner there. That's where my ex-wife used to wait for me."

"Thank you," I say.

"No problem. Just pay it forward, next time you see someone with a girlfriend like yours. Folks like us gotta stick together."

"I will, but she's not my girlfriend. She's my . . . I don't know. I don't know what she is."

"A monster, looks like." Frank's eyes glitter.

順子

[The Obedient Child]

You, 古田順子—you were real, and you lived. For a while. If your life had unfolded as it should have, I would not know your name. But now, across the world, you are "Junko Furuta"—Japanese contorted into foreign sounds and arranged in the wrong order. You have been reduced to the part of your life you had the least power to predict: your abduction, your captivity, your rape, your torture, your murder. You're the "girl" in the "concrete-encased high school girl murder case," the 女子高生 in the 女子高生コンクリート詰め殺人事件.

Here is what is known about you:

Your parents didn't name you with strange syllables. They called you 順子, "Obedient Child." For seventeen years, every letter, every roll call, paid homage to your obedience. Before your eighteenth birthday, on your way home from school, one boy kicked you off your bike, and the other offered you help. And you, Obedient Child, accepted. You didn't know they were both yakuza. You didn't know that what would happen in the forty days to follow would make me nauseous fifty years after and 7,000 miles away. It's known that, by the end, it was only the rotting smell of your still-living body that kept their hands off you.

Here is what I think I know about you:

There is a story online about the mahjong game the boys made you play. According to the story, you were not so Obedient. You refused to let them win, moving tiles with your broken fingers, and in their anger they lit you on fire. The fire part is true—the mahjong thing may not be. Someday, I predict, this mahjong game that may not have happened will play a vital part of the ghost story that you will become.

You will be 麻雀女, the Mahjong Woman, a wraith of Japan like Kuchisake-onna, Teke-teke, and Hanako-san. What real suffering underlies the stories of your restless sisters? No one remembers. Someday, you will also be the monster of your story, everyone's worst fear cast in human form. Hiding in shadows untouched by the neon lights of Tōkyō, challenging lone men with dark hearts to games of mahjong they will never win. Lighting them up like paper lanterns when they don't. Men will think you are the scary one, but women know better. Women will not fear you; they fear the boys who turn girls into ghosts.

Here is what I imagine about you:

As you rode your bike for the last time, I imagine you must have smelled like roses, because that's what I smelled like. In your shower I see the same pink plastic bottle that sat in mine on the nights I didn't come home. The only difference is the Japanese label. I never forget your age, because I was also seventeen. Did they trap you in a basement, too? Did the cold of the cinderblock walls soak through your naked skin? Did you see the spiders, tiny and delicate, watching with many eyes from deep corners?

I did. Bent over the back of a couch, throat raw with alcohol I did not want, but obediently drank. My spider was beautiful, the only lovely thing in an ugly moment—in an ugly summer. I studied her like I would die if I looked away. The scent of roses dripping out of my hair and catching in her web. With mercy and love, she turned me to unfeeling stone with her black pearl gaze. Blessed me with a body made of edged flint, harder and sharper than flesh. When the next man seized me, I imagined my skin opening into many jagged mouths and crushing his slithery fingers inside.

I am not Charis—not Graceful—anymore. I am the monster whose skin chews through bone. I am Medusa with spider legs for hair. Sadako, crawling on my belly through dark basement doors someone should have closed. I am not you, Miss Furuta—a real child subjected to horrors I cannot imagine—but when the Mahjong Woman challenges another cocksure stud to a game, I'll share her satisfaction in victory.

About Etchings Press

Etchings Press is a student-run publisher at the University of Indianapolis that runs a post-publication award—the Whirling Prize—as well as an annual publication contest for one poetry chapbook, one prose chapbook, and one novella. On occasion, Etchings Press publishes new chapbooks from previous winners. For more information about these contests and the Whirling Prize post-publication award, please visit etchings.uindy.edu.

Poetry
2024: *Elliott* by Brian Muriel
2023: *Other Side of Sea* by Xiaoqiu Qiu
2022: *A Place That Knows You* by Tiwaladeoluwa Adekunle
2022: *The Vaudeville Horse* by Elizabeth Kerlikowske
2021: *My Mother's Ghost Scrubs the Floor at 2 a.m.* by Robert Okaji
2020: *Vaginas Need Air* by Tori Grant Welhouse
2019: *As Lovers Always Do* by Marne Wilson
2018: *In the Herald of Improbable Misfortunes* by Robert Campbell
2017: *Uncle Harold's Maxwell House Haggadah* by Danny Caine
2016: *Some Animals* by Kelli Allen
2015: *Velocity of Slugs* by Joey Connelly
2014: *Action at a Distance* by Christopher Petruccelli

Prose
2024: *We Obedient Children* by Karris Rae (fiction and nonfiction hybrid)
2023: *Leaving the House Unlocked* by Elizabeth Enochs (nonfiction)
2022: *Triple Point* by Laura Story Johnson (essays)
2021: *Bad Man Love Stories* by Curtis VanDonkelaar (fiction)
2020: *Three in the Morning and You Don't Smoke Anymore* by Peter J. Stavros (fiction)
2019: *Dissenting Opinion from the Committee for the Beatitudes* by Marc J. Sheehan (fiction)

2018: *The Forsaken* by Chad V. Broughman (fiction)
2017: *Unravelings* by Sarah Cheshire (memoir)
2016: *Pathetic* by Shannon McLeod (essays)
2015: *Ologies* by Chelsea Biondolillo (essays)
2014: *Static: Stories* by Frederick Pelzer (fiction)

Novella
2024: *Pineville Trace* by Wes Blake
2023: *Our Cadaver* by Elizabeth Toman
2022: *Goodbye to the Ocean* by Susan L. Lin
2021: *Miss Alma May Learns to Fight* by Stuart Rose
2020: *Under Black Leaves* by Doug Ramspeck
2019: *Savonne, Not Vonny* by Robin Lee Lovelace
2018: *Edge of the Known Bus* Line by James R. Gapinski
2017: *The Denialist's Almanac* of American Plague and Pestilence
by Christopher Mohar
2016: *Followers* by Adam Fleming Petty

Chapbooks from Previous Winners
2022: *slighted...* by Chad V. Broughman (fiction)
2020: *Fruit Rot* by James R. Gapinski (fiction)
2016: *#LOVESONG* by Chelsea Biondolillo (microessays with
photos and found text)

Karris Rae is a fiction MFA/MA candidate at McNeese State University. She is also a fiction co-editor for T*he McNeese Review* and managing editor for *Boudin*. Her short work has appeared in *Metaphorosis Magazine, Reápparition Journal, The Chamber Magazine, The NoSleep Podcast*, and *Free Flash Fiction*, and is forthcoming in *50 Give or Take, Fourth Genre Magazine, Mount Hope Magazine*, and *Gargoyle Online*. Visit her website at karrisrae.com for more information.